little Miss Tiny

by Roger Hargreaves

Little Miss Tiny was extremely small.

Not very tall at all!

She was so very tiny she didn't live in a house.

Do you know where she lived?

In a mousehole, in the dining room of
Home Farm.

She had made the mousehole quite comfortable really, and luckily there weren't any mice because the farm cat had chased them all away.

The trouble was, because she was so tiny, nobody knew she lived there.

Nobody had noticed her.

Not even the farmer and his wife.

So, there she lived.

All alone.

With nobody to talk to.

She was very lonely.

And sad.

Oh dear!

One day she was feeling so lonely she decided to be very brave and go for a walk.

Out of her mousehole she came.

She crept across the dining room and went through the crack in the door and into the hall.

To Little Miss Tiny the hall looked as big as a field, and she scuttled across it to the back door of the farm.

Luckily for her the letterbox was at the bottom of the door and she squeezed herself through it and onto the doorstep.

It was all very exciting!

There before her was the farmyard.

She went exploring.

She came to a door with a gap at the bottom, and ducked in underneath.

There, inside, was a pig.

A large pig!

And, if you're as small as Little Miss Tiny, a large pig looks very large indeed.

Miss Tiny looked at the pig.

"Oink," he grunted, and moved closer to inspect this little person who had entered his sty.

"Oh my goodness me," squeaked Little Miss Tiny in alarm, and shot out of the pigsty as fast as ever her little legs would carry her.

Which wasn't very fast beacuse her legs were so very little!

She ran right around to the back of the pigsty before she stopped.

She leaned against the wall and put her hands over her eyes, and tried to get her breath back.

Suddenly, she heard a noise.

A very close noise.

A sort of breathing noise.

Very close indeed!

Oh!

She hardly dared take her hands away from her eyes, but when she did she wished she hadn't.

What do you think it was, there, right in front of her, looking at her with green eyes?

Ginger!

The farm cat!!

Poor Little Miss Tiny.

Ginger grinned, showing his teeth.

"HELP!" shrieked Miss Tiny at the top of her voice.

"Oh somebody please HELP!"

The trouble was, the top of Little Miss Tiny's voice was not a very loud place.

Ginger grinned another grin.

Every day Mr Strong went to Home Farm to buy some eggs.

He liked eggs.

Lots of them.

That day he was walking home across the farmyard when he heard a very tiny squeak.

He stopped.

There it was again.

Round the corner.

He looked round the corner and saw Ginger and the poor trapped Little Miss Tiny.

"SHOO!" said Mr Strong to Ginger, and picked up Little Miss Tiny.

Very gently.

"Hello," he said. "Who are you?"

"I'm... I'm... I'm... Miss Tiny."

"You are, aren't you?" smiled Mr Strong. "Well, if I was as tiny as you, I wouldn't go wandering around large farmyards!"

"But..." said Miss Tiny, and told Mr Strong about how she was so lonely she had to come out to find somebody to talk to.

"Oh dear," said Mr Strong. "Well now, let's see if we can't find you some friends to talk to."

And now, every week, Mr Strong collects Little Miss Tiny and takes her off to see her friends.

Three weeks ago he took her to see Mr Funny, who told her so many jokes she just couldn't stop laughing all day.

Two weeks ago he took her to see Mr Greedy.

He told her his recipe for his favourite meal.

"But that's much much too much for tiny little me," she laughed.

Mr Greedy grinned.

"For you," he said, "divide by a hundred!"

Last week Mr Strong took her to see Mr Silly.

And Mr Silly showed her how to stand on your head.

"That's very silly," giggled Little Miss Tiny.

"Thank you," replied Mr Silly, modestly.

And guess who she met this week?

Somebody who's become a special little friend.

"I never thought I'd ever meet anybody
smaller than myself," laughed Mr Small.

Little Miss Tiny looked up at him, and smiled.

"You wait till I grow up," she said.

Fantastic offers for Little Miss fans!

Collect all your Mr. Men or Little Miss books in these superb durable collectors' cases!
Only £5.99 inc. postage and packing, these wipe-clean, hard-wearing cases will give all your Mr. Men or Little Miss books a beautiful new home!

Keep track of your collection with this giant-sized double-sided Mr. Men and Little Miss Collectors' poster.
Collect 6 tokens and we will send you a brilliant giant-sized double-sided collectors' poster! Simply tape a £1 coin to cover postage and packing in the space provided and fill out the form overleaf.

STICK £1 COIN HERE
(for poster only)

Only need a few Little Miss or Mr. Men to complete your set? You can order any of the titles on the back of the books from our Mr. Men order line on 0870 787 1724. Orders should be delivered between 5 and 7 working days.

--- TO BE COMPLETED BY AN ADULT ---

To apply for any of these great offers, ask an adult to complete the details below and send this whole page with the appropriate payment and tokens, to: MR. MEN CLASSIC OFFER, PO BOX 715, HORSHAM RH12 5WG

☐ Please send me a giant-sized double-sided collectors' poster.
AND ☐ I enclose 6 tokens and have taped a £1 coin to the other side of this page.

☐ Please send me ☐ Mr. Men Library case(s) and/or ☐ Little Miss library case(s) at £5.99 each inc P&P

☐ I enclose a cheque/postal order payable to Egmont UK Limited for £...............

OR ☐ Please debit my MasterCard / Visa / Maestro / Delta account (delete as appropriate) for £...............

Card no. ☐☐☐☐ ☐☐☐☐ ☐☐☐☐ ☐☐☐☐ ☐☐☐☐   Security code ☐☐☐

Issue no. (if available) ☐   Start Date ☐☐/☐☐/☐☐   Expiry Date ☐☐/☐☐/☐☐

Fan's name: ....   Date of birth: ....

Address: ....

....

Postcode: ....

Name of parent / guardian: ....

Email for parent / guardian: ....

Signature of parent / guardian: ....

Please allow 28 days for delivery. Offer is only available while stocks last. We reserve the right to change the terms of this offer at any time and we offer a 14 day money back guarantee. This does not affect your statutory rights. Offers apply to UK only.

☐ We may occasionally wish to send you information about other Egmont children's books. If you would rather we didn't, please tick this box.

Ref: LIM 001